J Kibbey

Kibbey, Marsha.

The helping place

© THE BAKER & TAYLOR CO.

The Helping Place

by Marsha Kibbey

illustrations by
Jennifer Hagerman

 Carolrhoda Books, Inc. / Minneapolis

Some of the words in this story are explained in
the glossary on the last page.

All of the characters and places in this book
are fictitious, and any resemblance to
actual persons or places is purely coincidental.

This book is available in two editions:
Library binding by Carolrhoda Books, Inc.
Soft cover by First Avenue Editions
241 First Avenue North
Minneapolis, MN 55401

Library of Congress Cataloging-in-Publication Data

Kibbey, Marsha.
    The helping place/by Marsha Kibbey; illustrations by Jennifer
Hagerman.
    p.   cm.
    Summary: A little girl's experiences when her grandmother
spends some time in a nursing home help her to have a better
feeling about those helping places.
    ISBN 0-87614-680-9 (lib. bdg.)
    ISBN 0-87614-557-8 (pbk.)
    [1. Nursing homes—Fiction. 2. Grandmothers—Fiction.]
I. Hagerman, Jennifer, ill. II. Title.
PZ7.K529He   1991   91-2826
[Fic]—dc20   CIP
                                                                AC

Manufactured in the United States of America

1 2 3 4 5 6 7 8 9 10 00 99 98 97 96 95 94 93 92 91

To the people who live and work in nursing homes.

I opened the door and yelled, "Mom, Grammy, I'm home."

But it was Dad's voice that called back, "Amy, I'm in here."

I dropped my backpack on the floor and rushed to the kitchen, asking, "Why are you home at this time of day? Where's Grammy and Mom?"

Dad frowned and said, "This morning, after you left for school, your grandmother fell. An ambulance took Grammy to the hospital, and Mom has been there with her most of the day."

I asked lots of questions about Grammy, but Dad didn't have any answers. He just said, "I'm sure the doctors are taking good care of her."

After Dad and I watched television for a while, I went to the bedroom that Grammy and I share. I did my homework while our cat, Patches, slept on Grammy's bed.

It was strange for Grammy to be gone. When Grammy came to live with us, I didn't think I would ever say I missed her, but I really did miss her that afternoon.

Grammy has a disease called Alzheimer's that makes her forgetful and confused. Sometimes she can't remember how to do simple things, like reading or telling time.

Mom and Dad didn't think it was safe for Grammy to live alone anymore, so she moved in with us.

When she came, I was angry because I had to share my bedroom with her. I got used to sharing my room, but I'll never get used to Grammy being different. It's so sad!

Grammy used to be so much fun. She was always cooking or quilting, and she loved to read. When we visited her on the farm where she and Grandpa lived, my favorite thing to do was sit on her lap and listen to her read to me. Now she can't read anymore because she can't always understand what the words mean.

Sometimes she sits in her rocking chair and stares at an open book, but she holds the book upside down. Mom and I think it makes Grammy feel good just to hold a book, so we don't say anything.

It's been hard learning to understand how Alzheimer's disease has changed the way Grammy's mind works, and to realize that she can't help the strange things she does and says.

Later that evening, Mom came home. She told us Grammy had a broken hip, and that the doctor would do surgery tomorrow to fix the break. She said I couldn't visit Grammy at the hospital because I'm not old enough.

For the next two weeks, during the day Mom visited Grammy at the hospital. After school, Mom and I visited nursing homes. The doctor told Mom and Grammy that Grammy would need to be moved to a nursing home to finish recovering from her broken hip.

Before we visited the first one, I asked Mom if a nursing home was a place where nurses live. Mom laughed and said, "No, it's a place almost like a hospital, where nurses take care of people who aren't well enough to live at home."

All the nursing homes seemed the same. Most of them have a dining room that looks like a big restaurant, a huge room with a television set and chairs, and an activity room. The activity room looks like our art room at school, and it has a piano.

The hallways are wide, and there are handrails on the walls. The people who can walk often use the handrails as they walk up and down the halls. Some people use wheelchairs or walkers to move around.

Most of the rooms where the people live are shared by two people. A few of the rooms are for only one person, but Mom says they cost a lot more money.

When we were looking at the nursing homes, all I could think was that I didn't want Grammy to stay in one of those places. Mom said, "Amy, I don't want her to stay there either, but right now we can't take care of her at home. The doctor says we should be able to bring Grammy home by Christmas, though."

We looked at lots of nursing homes. We talked with some of the people who live there. We also talked with the nurses. We looked at the residents' rooms and met with the administrator, the person who runs the nursing home.

Even though all the nursing homes seemed alike, we chose The Helping Place, because it's close to where we live. The people who work there were kind to the residents, the building was clean, and the food was tasty.

The day before the doctor said that Grammy needed to leave the hospital, we took her rocking chair, the quilt from her bed, and some of her clothes to the nursing home. The room looked a little better with Grammy's things there.

The next day when I came home from school Mom had taken Grammy to the nursing home. I wanted to visit her, but Mom said that Mrs. Graves, the administrator, had asked us to wait two days before we came to visit.

Finally, after school on Friday, Mom and I went to visit Grammy. We walked down the long hallway and stopped at the nurses' station near Grammy's room. The station was at the end of a large room where some of the residents were watching television. The nurses were very busy.

Mom asked, "How is Mrs. Clark doing?"

One of the nurses smiled and said, "She's settling in nicely, but she's been asking for someone named Amy."

Before Mom had a chance to say anything, I said, "That's me!"

The nurse looked at me with a smile and said, "Good. She'll be very glad to see you. Go right on down to her room."

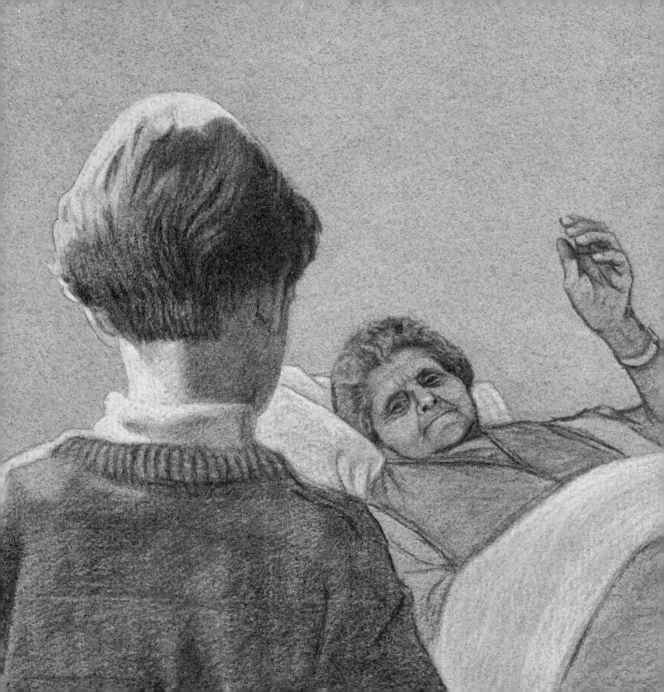

I was so excited as we walked down the hallway! When we got to the room, Grammy was looking out the window. Mom called, "Hello," and Grammy looked toward the door. Our eyes met, and she reached her hands toward me.

She tried to sit up, but she couldn't. She was fastened to the bed with a strange-looking vest.

I ran toward the bed and we hugged each other for a long, long time. It felt so good to have Grammy's arms around me. But it made me sad to think that she had to be in a strange place and couldn't get out of bed.

I sat at the foot of the bed while Mom talked to Grammy. Grammy kept telling Mom she wanted to go home. Grammy was upset, but as usual, Mom did a good job of calming her down.

Soon it was time to leave. The minute we were in the hall I said, "Mom, why is Grammy tied to the bed?"

Mom answered very quickly, "Amy, it's necessary for Grammy's safety. Let's stop in the office and see if Mrs. Graves can explain some of the things we find so new."

As we walked down the hall toward the office, I noticed two people sitting on a bench near the front door. They were holding their hats and coats. While we waited for Mrs. Graves, we sat down next to them.

"Do you live here?" I asked one of them.

She said, "Yes, but we are going out. Our friend is coming to get us."

Finally, Mrs. Graves invited us into her office. She said, "I'm sure you both have questions for me. Where would you like to begin?"

I spoke before Mom had a chance. "Why is Grammy tied to the bed?" I asked.

Mrs. Graves looked right into my eyes and said, "I know the idea of a loved one being tied in a bed is upsetting, Amy, but it is necessary. The vest is called a posey or a restraint. Because of your grandmother's Alzheimer's disease, there is a chance she might become confused and try to get out of bed without someone helping her. If she gets up by herself, she might fall and hurt her hip again."

Mom asked other questions, but all I could think about was the posey, and Grammy having to stay in the nursing home. I knew she didn't like being there. I thought it might help if I came by after school to visit with Grammy.

My friend Mary and I always walk home from school together, so before we left, I asked Mrs. Graves if Mary and I could visit with Grammy on our way home from school.

Mrs. Graves said, "Amy, you're welcome to visit anytime your mother gives you permission. I know all of the residents will be glad to see you and your friend."

The next morning, I asked Mom if Mary and I could visit Grammy on our way home from school. Mom said, "Sure, but let me telephone Mary's mom and make sure it's all right with her."

I went upstairs, found a deck of cards, and tossed them into my backpack. Grammy likes to play gin rummy. When I came downstairs, Mom said it was fine for us to stop by the nursing home.

After school, Mary and I went to visit Grammy. She was very quiet, so Mary and I did most of the talking. Grammy was sitting in a big chair with a tray that looked kind of like a high chair for big people. The nurse told us the chair was called a geri-chair. We used the tray to hold our cards when we played gin rummy.

Mary began talking to Grammy's roommate. Her name is Nell, and she talks more than Grammy. She smiles a lot, too. She told Mary she used to be a teacher, and Mary told her about our day at school.

Nell told us about life in the nursing home while Grammy sat silently and listened. Nell said that Sunday is her favorite day because more people come to visit.

As we were leaving, we decided to ask Mrs. Graves what was wrong with Grammy's roommate. Mrs. Graves was talking to those people who are always sitting near the office. This time they were wearing their hats and coats.

When we asked Mrs. Graves if we could talk to her, she said, "Certainly, go on into the office." A few minutes later, she came in and asked, "What can I do for you?" I introduced Mary and told Mrs. Graves we wondered what was wrong with Nell.

Mrs. Graves said, "Girls, Nell had a stroke. A stroke happens in the brain, and it can make part of the body paralyzed—unable to move. Nell's stroke paralyzed the left side of her body."

I asked about the people with the hats and coats. Mrs. Graves said, "Age and disease affect different people in different ways, girls. I don't have an exact explanation for what's wrong with those two people, but their minds don't work quite right anymore. You see, they think someone is coming to take them somewhere. Since they're happy sitting and waiting, we let them."

When we left, we said good-bye to the people with the hats and coats. They waved to us and smiled. That was the first time we had seen them smile.

Two months passed. Mary and I stopped at the nursing home many afternoons on our way home from school. Being with Grammy was great, and we made lots of new friends at the nursing home.

One of them was a man named Bill, who was recovering from a stroke, like Nell. Bill liked to play cards, but he couldn't hold the cards in his hand. Mary and I cut slits in a shoe box so the box could hold Bill's cards. Bill taught us how to play crazy eights. It was fun learning a new card game.

Nell helped Mary with her math, and Mary's math grade rose from a C to an A. Sometimes I wrote notes for some of the residents who couldn't write anymore for one reason or another.

Some of the women had their hair done at the beauty shop in the nursing home. Sometimes we painted their fingernails after they had their hair done.

A few times we took Patches for a visit, and everyone was always glad to see him. Grammy's eyes seemed to sparkle when Patches found his favorite napping place—in Grammy's rocking chair.

Sometimes we sang songs like "Row, Row, Row Your Boat" and "Oh! Susannah." As it got close to Christmas, we sang carols, and everyone liked that very much.

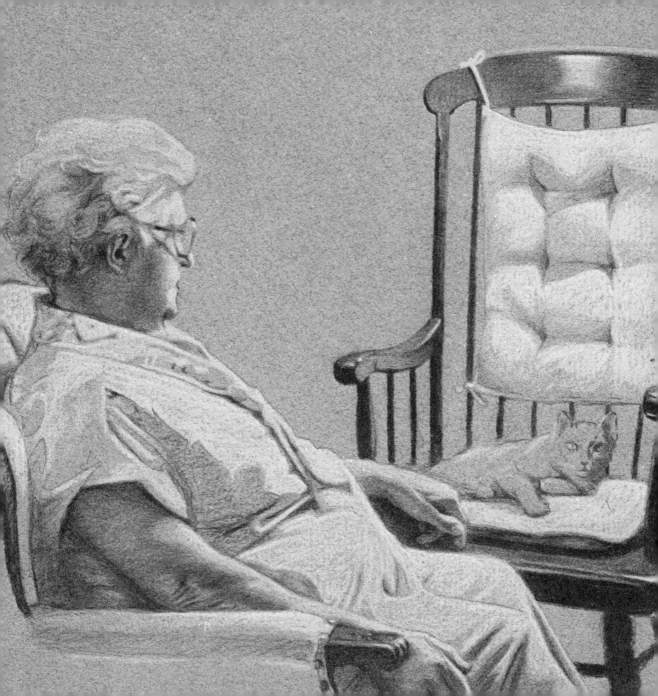

One week before Christmas, Grammy was well enough to come home. Dad moved her things back into our room. She had to be careful when she moved around, and she had to use a walker. We had to help her a lot, but we didn't mind. We were glad to have her back home.

Mary and I still stop by The Helping Place on our way home from school to visit our old friends. Everyone there is always glad to see us. Bill is teaching Mary and me another new card game, and Nell still helps Mary with her math. Nell has a new roommate now.

When Grammy broke her hip, I was upset because she had to live in a nursing home. Now I see why nursing homes are important. I'm glad Grammy is home with us now, but I'm also glad The Helping Place was there when she needed it.

Glossary

Alzheimer's disease:
a disease of the brain that causes confusion, forgetfulness, and other problems

geri-chair: a large moveable chair with a tray across the arms

nursing home: a place where elderly people or people recovering from an illness stay when they cannot be cared for at home

posey: a vest or jacket that keeps people from getting up from a bed or chair. Also called a restraint.

recovering: getting better after an illness

resident: a person who lives in a particular place, such as a nursing home

stroke: the human body's reaction to the bursting of a blood vessel or artery in the brain

walker: a metal device used to help people walk